Dear Parents,

Welcome to the Scholastic Reader se
years of experience with teachers, p it
into a program that is designed to match your child's interests
and skills.

Level 1—Short sentences and stories made up of words kids
can sound out using their phonics skills and words that are
important to remember.

Level 2—Longer sentences and stories with words kids need
to know and new "big" words that they will want to know.

Level 3—From sentences to paragraphs to longer stories, these
books have large "chunks" of texts and are made up of a rich
vocabulary.

Level 4—First chapter books with more words and fewer
pictures.

It is important that children learn to read well enough to succeed
in school and beyond. Here are ideas for reading this book with
your child:

- Look at the book together. Encourage your child to read the
  title and make a prediction about the story.
- Read the book together. Encourage your child to sound out
  words when appropriate. When your child struggles, you can
  help by providing the word.
- Encourage your child to retell the story. This is a great way
  to check for comprehension.
- Have your child take the fluency test on the last page to check
  progress.

Scholastic Readers are designed to support your child's efforts
to learn how to read at every age and every stage.
Enjoy helping your child learn to read and love to read.

    —**Francie Alexander**
       Chief Education Officer
       Scholastic Education

Copyright © 2003 by DC Comics.
Batman and all related characters and elements
are trademarks of and © DC Comics.
All rights reserved. Published by Scholastic Inc.
SCHOLASTIC, CARTWHEEL BOOKS, and associated logos are
trademarks and/or registered trademarks of Scholastic Inc.

Library of Congress Cataloging-in-Publication Data

McCann, Jesse Leon
     Batman: time thaw / by Jesse Leon McCann; illustrated by
John Byrne.
     p.   cm. — (Scholastic readers. level 3)
"Cartwheel Books"
Summary: When Gotham City is invaded by prehistoric animals,
Batman comes to the rescue.
ISBN 0-439-47096-X (pbk)
[1. Prehistoric animals — Fiction. 2. Heroes — Fiction.] I. Title: time
thaw. II. Byrne, John, 1950 – ill. III. Title IV. Series
PZ7.G79915Bat 2003
[E] — dc21   2003004928

10 9 8 7 6 5   04 05 06 07

Printed in China 67 • First printing, September 2003

Written by **Jesse Leon McCann**

Illustrated by **John Byrne**

Batman created by Bob Kane

Scholastic Reader — Level 3

SCHOLASTIC INC.

New York Toronto London Auckland Sydney
Mexico City New Delhi Hong Kong Buenos Aires

CHAPTER ONE

CREATURE FEATURE

Bruce Wayne was one of the richest men in Gotham City. He lived in Wayne Manor, above a secret cave—the Batcave!

That's because Bruce was also Batman!

Every evening Batman carefully checked his crime-fighting tools and equipment. Tonight he was almost ready to go out on patrol.

A STRANGE *FOG* HAD COVERED *GOTHAM CITY.*

It was a cold night in Gotham City. Police detectives Harvey Bullock and Renee Montoya shivered inside their squad car.

They were not happy. A strange fog had covered Gotham the last three nights. The fog was very cold and thick. And every cop had to work long hours.

THOOM!

Montoya's eyes grew wide. "What was that?"

THOOM! THOOM! The ground shook.

"Good question!" Bullock said. He quickly wiped the window with a rag.

They looked out into the soupy fog. What they saw was chilling. Very big creatures were coming at them from the mist!

THOOM! THOOM! THOOM!

And then . . . *CRUNCH!*

One huge beast stepped on the front of their car. It crushed the hood flat.

"Holy cow!" Bullock jumped from the car. "Get out, Montoya! That thing isn't going around us!"

Montoya rolled out onto the cold street. She looked back to see the creature wreck their car . . . *CRUNCH! CRUNCH!* Then it went on down the road.

The two detectives rubbed their eyes.

They watched the beasts disappear into the fog.

The enormous creatures looked like mastodons, giant sloths, and woolly mammoths! But those prehistoric creatures had been extinct for thousands of years—since the Ice Age!

CHAPTER TWO

FOG FACTORY

ABOARD THE BATPLANE, *BATMAN* INVESTIGATES...

THIS FOG WAS NOT NATURAL!

As the mist rolled in for a third night, Batman the Dark Knight was in his Batplane. He was flying over the ocean.

Batman knew something was wrong. He had been checking the weather satellite all day. It was always the same: Clear. But this fog was not natural!

The fog was coming from the east. That part of the ocean was dotted with small islands. Maybe these islands held the answer to the fog.

Sure enough, on one rocky island, he spotted a huge factory. Several smokestacks poured out big clouds of thick, cold, man-made fog.

The only place to land was the factory's roof. Batman turned on the landing gear and set the plane down.

He stepped outside the plane. Frost crunched under his boots. The smokestacks were covered with four inches of ice!

Just then Batman's radio buzzed. Commissioner Gordon was calling him.

"Batman, it's the craziest thing," Commissioner Gordon said. "We've been

invaded—by a pack of prehistoric animals.

We need you!"

"I'll be there in fifteen minutes."

Batman turned back to the Batplane.

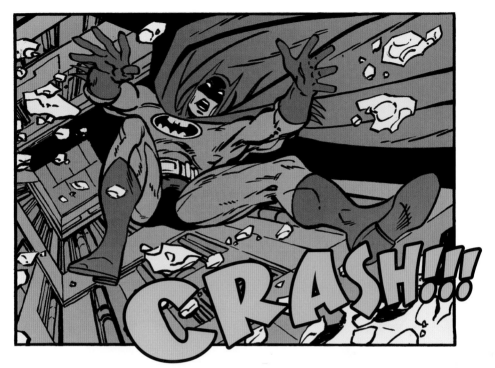

The mystery of the fog-making factory would have to wait!

But he didn't reach the Batplane.

Suddenly, a trap door in the roof opened under him and he was falling! *WHOMP!* He landed on a cold concrete floor.

"Ah, Batman. I thought it was you. Welcome!"

Batman knew that voice.

It was Mr. Freeze!

CHAPTER THREE

FAREWELL, BATMAN!

Batman got to his feet. "What's this about, Mr. Freeze?" he asked.

Mr. Freeze was on a platform twenty feet above the ground. He looked down meanly at the Dark Knight.

"Revenge, my old enemy...for what has been done to my life!"

Mr. Freeze was once a scientist named Dr. Victor Fries. He did experiments in super-cold temperatures. But a laboratory accident had changed Fries. He now needed to live in a special freezing cold suit.

Dr. Fries became Mr. Freeze! He turned to crime to pay for his plans to turn Gotham City into an icy, frozen land.

"I'm sure you've heard about the strange creatures in your foggy city," Freeze said. He pushed a button on a panel. The lights inside the factory went on.

"I was lucky to find my prehistoric friends during a recent dig in Siberia," Freeze said with a laugh.

Batman looked around. He knew he

GOTHAM
WILL
FREEZE!

CLICK!

would have to fight soon—possibly for

his life. So he used this time to listen

and prepare.

"I was digging for a special diamond, the

Sol Stone," Freeze went on. "It's the last

piece I need for my laser-pulse ice cannon."

Freeze pushed another button. Beneath

him, the floor opened. A hovercraft rose to

ground level. On it was a huge, dangerous

looking cannon.

"One blast and Gotham City will freeze

forever," Freeze said. He stepped onto the

hovercraft. "However, I didn't find the Sol Stone—just creatures frozen for thousands of years. Now they and my freezing fog will keep the police busy while I finally get my Sol Stone!"

ON THE *HOVERCRAFT* WAS A *DANGEROUS LOOKING CANNON!*

"By stealing it!" Batman said.

"An excellent guess, Batman," the cold criminal laughed. "How lucky for me it's on display at the Gotham Museum."

Mr. Freeze flipped a switch. A part of the wall to the outside opened. Batman ran after the hovercraft.

Mr. Freeze flipped another switch. Another part of the wall opened. Out leaped two giant, snarling creatures.

Saber-toothed tigers!

"Farewell, Batman!" Freeze steered the craft outside. The wall began to close behind him. "Play nicely with my pets!"

Now Batman was alone with the circling tigers. He stayed still. The tigers would leap at the slightest move.

Batman reached slowly for his utility belt.

That was all it took.

GROWL!

A tiger roared and leaped. It hit Batman hard, knocking him backward!

Batman back-flipped away from the tiger's slashing claws. With his last flip, he leaped over the growling beast.

The second cat was waiting. Batman was forced to kick it in the head. The tiger was briefly stunned. Then Batman ran as fast as he could toward Mr. Freeze's platform.

But the tigers were faster. One of them slammed him down from behind. Batman rolled onto his back as the cat slashed at him with razor-sharp claws.

Would that moment be the end of the Dark Knight?

CHAPTER FOUR

A QUIET MIST

In one quick move, Batman grabbed a
mask and gas capsule from his utility belt.
He covered his mouth and nose with the
mask. Then he threw the capsule to the floor.
A thick mist rose from the capsule.

THE KNOCKOUT GAS HAD WORKED!

The two giant cats keeled over and passed out. The knockout gas had worked!

The sleeping tigers were now as harmless as kittens. Batman climbed to the roof. Mr. Freeze was way ahead of him—and Batman needed to get to the Batplane as soon as possible!

Batman skidded to a stop on the icy roof. He saw that Mr. Freeze had done one last thing before escaping.

The Batplane's engines were frozen solid!

CHAPTER FIVE

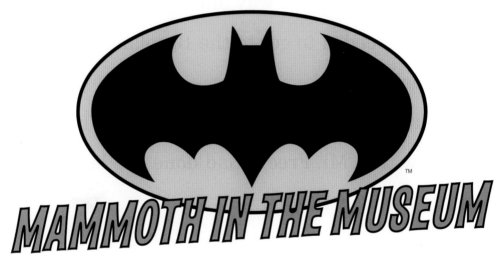

MAMMOTH IN THE MUSEUM

Mr. Freeze had planned perfectly. No one paid attention as he froze the Gotham City Museum's alarm system. Then he flew his hovercraft through the big doors of the museum's loading dock.

Inside, Freeze found the Sol Stone. He had to be careful. If he set off a different special alarm, a cage would drop over the display case. And that would trap him.

Luckily, a quick blast from his freeze gun silenced the alarm. The Sol Stone was his!

Mr. Freeze smashed the glass display and grabbed the big diamond. With this, his cannon's laser would be much more powerful. Soon, Gotham City would be in ice forever!

The Sol Stone was beautiful, as delicate as a snowflake. He held it up to admire it. And then...

FWHAAP!

A Batarang hit Freeze's wrist! The Sol Stone went flying. It was snatched from the air by a gloved hand.

The villain was shocked to see Batman.
The Dark Knight was riding one of Freeze's
own woolly mammoths!

"What?" Freeze raged. "How?"

BATMAN HAD *WHISKED* TOWARD GOTHAM CITY IN HIS *BATGLIDER.*

Batman almost smiled. There was no need to tell the villain the truth. When he saw the Batplane had been frozen, Batman had thought of another way to leave the island!

Climbing into the cockpit, the Dark Knight strapped on his Batglider. Then he pulled the airplane's ejector-seat lever. With a blast, he was shot straight up, high into the night sky!

His Batglider wings opened. As the wind filled them, he whisked toward Gotham City. During his flight, he called his trusted aide, Alfred.

"Prepare a barrel of sleeping gas," Batman ordered.

When he landed, Batman quickly found a fire truck. He then attached a hose to the knockout gas. Driving around town, Batman used the sleeping gas on all the giant prehistoric animals. Before long, they were snoozing peacefully in the streets.

He found the last mammoth outside the Gotham Museum…but his knockout gas was gone! Luckily, as millionaire Bruce Wayne, Batman had ridden elephants many times on safari in India. Batman rode the huge beast into the museum. And that's when he met up again with Mr. Freeze.

But Mr. Freeze didn't even wait for Batman to answer. He raised his freeze gun and growled, "You've been so worried about my big freeze gun, you've forgotten about this little one!"

THE DARK KNIGHT RODE THE *HUGE BEAST* INTO THE *MUSEUM.*

CHAPTER SIX

A FREEZING FIGHT

Mr. Freeze shot Batman with a blast from his freeze gun. Batman was trapped from the shoulders down in solid ice.

BATMAN FELL TO THE FLOOR...FROZEN!

He fell to the floor at the mammoth's feet.

The Sol Stone dropped to the ground. Mr. Freeze snatched it up and returned to his ice cannon. "Once the gem is in place, I will be unstoppable!" he shouted.

Batman had to act quickly. He rolled his ice-covered body into the mammoth's foot. The creature lifted its foot and then stepped on him, cracking open the ice! Before the beast's foot could hurt him, Batman quickly rolled out from under it.

Mr. Freeze was fitting the diamond into his cannon. Batman jumped across the room, tackling the villain. The startled Mr. Freeze struggled as Batman quickly tied him with his Batrope. Batman plucked the Sol Stone from the ice cannon. Freeze's plot was over!

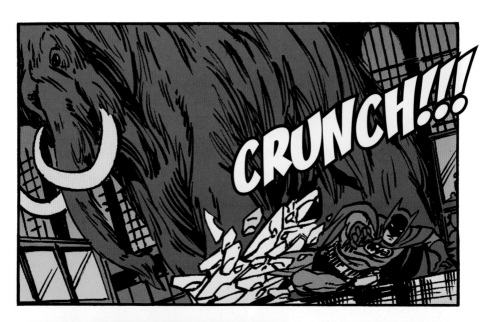

Later, Batman—now dressed as Bruce Wayne—and Alfred sat by a crackling fire in the parlor of Wayne Manor. They watched the fog outside the windows slowly disappear.

Batman had made sure Mr. Freeze was safely with the police. The deadly ice cannon was in pieces. Then Batman had returned to the island and destroyed Freeze's fog factory.

"I heard the prehistoric creatures have found a new home in the Gotham Zoo," Alfred said. He poured more hot tea. "A fine and chilly night's work, Master Bruce."

"Yes, Alfred," Bruce smiled. "But nothing warms me more than knowing Gotham City is safe."

Fluency Fun

The words in each list below end in the same sounds.
Read the words in a list.
Read them again.
Read them faster.
Try to read all 15 words in one minute.

carefully	**craziest**	**circling**
deadly	**foggiest**	**fighting**
perfectly	**luckiest**	**freezing**
possibly	**richest**	**laughing**
woolly	**slightest**	**snarling**

Look for these words in the story.

equipment	**detectives**	**creatures**
extinct	**island**	

Note to Parents:

According to *A Dictionary of Reading and Related Terms*, fluency is "the ability to read smoothly, easily, and readily with freedom from word-recognition problems." Fluency is necessary for good comprehension and enjoyable reading. The activities on this page include a speed drill and a sight-recognition drill. Speed drills build fluency because they help students rapidly recognize common syllables and spelling patterns in words, and they're fun! Sight-recognition drills help students smoothly and accurately recognize words. Practice these activities with your child to help him or her become a fluent reader.

—**Wiley Blevins**,
Reading Specialist